Christmas 2016

Past th
Trib
and Straight on to
Derring Do

To Thomas 2016

Hilary Orme

ISBN-13: 978-1367408463
ISBN-10: 1367408466

Dedicated to Diane Edwards and Megan Jackson in response to their requests to, "tell me another", albiet fifty years apart.

Cover design by Rebecca Jackson of Feathertree

Chapter 1

Tina the Tiny Terror would be in the corner of the playground, telling everyone about the two weeks she had spent in her parents' timeshare in Tenerife. Monty Moira would top that with stories about her summer in the family villa in Barbados and all the rich and famous people she had spotted, but Ginny Mac would be most admired. She would have had two holidays - one with her mum and step dad and another with her dad and step mum. I was dreading the first day of term, when my friends would ask, "And where have you been, Meg?"

Last year, I had just managed to impress them with my visit to the Hay Festival with Ma. None of my friends had ever heard of it, but thought that going to a festival sounded quite a grown up thing to do. I had met a few celebrities and was able to show them a book signed by the man who read the news on Breakfast Television. This year, there was no way that I would be able to make, "I spent the whole six weeks with my Grandma," sound the slightest bit exciting.

Ma had been ill and was due to start her treatment during the following week, so Aunt Hattie had arrived a few days before the end of term. She was an organiser by nature and had soon set about sorting my clothes into neat piles and packing them in the large red suitcase that we kept under the bed, just in case we ever had the opportunity to go somewhere exotic. I watched my aunt folding, rolling and smoothing T shirts and trousers, pants and pyjamas.

Satisfied with the result, she closed the case and announced, "I could pack for England!" I nodded, unsure of exactly what she meant, but certain that it was something to be proud of.

"Strange sayings run in our family," Ma had told me one day. Grandma had just that minute said that someone had a voice that was so shrill that it sounded like 'a glead under the door'. I had looked puzzled, as I had no idea what a 'glead' could be and what it was doing under a door.

"Better not ask," Ma had said and had just rolled her eyes and shook her head. So I never did ask, but instead tried to work out what Grandma and Aunt Hattie meant when they said unusual things. Sometimes I got it right, but most of the time I got it wrong.

As Aunt Hattie stood back to admire how well she had packed the case, I took a deep breath and plucked up the courage to ask, "Do I have to go? I wouldn't be any trouble and I could help to look after Ma. I know where everything is in the house and ...."

I had tried to put on my most pleading voice, but my aunt said that I was just "wheedling", whatever that might be. With a sigh, she moved the case onto the floor and then patted the space it had occupied on the bed, "Come and sit next to me. I need to talk to you." I knew that they wanted me to go to Grandma's, because Ma would be very tired, but Aunt Hattie tried the trick that grown ups use when they want you to do something: She made me feel guilty.

"Since Grandma has been on her own, she's been very lonely, you know. She's been looking forward to your staying with her so much. When I saw her last week, she showed me the new bed covers she had bought for your bed in the spare room. Lovely florals! 'Meg's too old for teddy bears now!', she had said."

I quietly folded my hands in my lap and looked down at them, "I suppose I could go for a short time. Perhaps a week or two and then ..."

Aunt Hattie took my hand and stroked it gently.

"I think you will need to stay for a little bit longer than that," she said reassuringly and then added brightly. "Besides, Grandma will bring you here every Friday for lunch. You'll like that, won't you?" She always seemed unsure if she had made herself clear as she was not very good with children. I thought that her awkwardness came about because she had been a child so long ago that she had forgotten what it was like. I gulped hard.

Struggling to hold back the tears, I realised that there was no hope of persuading Ma or Aunt Hattie to change their minds so answered feebly, "Yes, I suppose so."

"What's more," added Aunt Hattie, "you'll get to see Grandma's mad cat!"

I managed a faint smile and had to agree that I was looking forward to seeing Dotty, the little Bengal cat.

On Saturday, we arrived at Grandma's house just before midday. Although it was less than an hour's drive from home, Ma's illness had made traveling difficult and as Grandma did not drive very much anymore, it had been a few months since my last visit. Graymalkin Cottage stood on top of a hill and as we got out of the car, I thought that if I tried very hard I would probably be able to see my house on a clear day. I made up my mind that I would try to do that every morning until it was time to go home for good at the end of the summer holidays.

I was deposited in the hallway along with my bags and Aunt Hattie made a speedy retreat. I was starting to feel sorry for myself and about to kick the red suitcase in revenge for not having taken me somewhere exotic, when Grandma appeared and thrust a picnic rug into my hands, collected a tray from the kitchen and went out into the garden. It was a warm day, so she told me to spread the rug on the grass under the apple tree, where there was some shade. A plate of ham sandwiches, dishes of strawberries and cream and a big jug of homemade lemonade were laid in the centre of the rug. There was a sudden rustling in the bushes nearby and out sprang a cat with a coat the colour of cinnamon, peppered all over with large nutmeg spots. As she moved into the sunlight, her fur looked as if it had been sprinkled with golden glitter and she announced her arrival with a cry that was half bark and half chirp.

"Dotty, you fusspot!" said Grandma as the cat rubbed against her, purring like a lawnmower. "Lured by ham

sandwiches, I think. I know this is just cupboard love!"
"Cupboard love?" I thought. "Better not ask!"
"She's beautiful!" I said and as if attracted by a fresh admirer, Dotty turned, excitedly swinging her long tail to and fro. With one swish, the jug was thrown into the air and as we ran for cover from the lemonade shower, Dotty retreated into the bushes with a ham sandwich in her mouth.
"Hmmm," said Grandma, "I'm not sure about that. 'Handsome is as handsome does'!"
"Better not ask," I thought.
The rest of the picnic continued undisturbed and Dotty did not appear again until later in the afternoon.
After Grandma had cleared away the remains of their meal and put the picnic blanket in the washing machine she said, "Now, we'd better get to work in the garden." I did not share my grandmother's enthusiasm for this activity. What Grandma referred to as "minibeasts", I called "creepy crawlies" and our first job did nothing to make me change my mind about the creatures that lived in the undergrowth.
"We'll start with the Hostas," said Grandma. "The slugs and snails have feasted on them this year!" Seeing the look of horror on my face, she added, "You can hold the bucket. I'll do the nasty part!"
Hostas had spade-shaped, green leaves that seemed to be particularly attractive to slugs and snails. I held a large metal bucket while my grandmother turned over leaf after leaf searching out the offenders and dropping them into it. Each snail fell to the bottom of the bucket with a loud clang. I hoped that she would

not take too long, as one or two of the larger creatures were already starting to make their way up the side.
"Look at my poor plant," said Grandma. "It's just like Raggedy Ann!" I didn't ask, but was beginning to suspect that even my grandmother did not know what half of her sayings meant.
A loud chirp from behind the Hostas, signalled the return of Dotty.
"That cat is too clever," said Grandma. "She knows what comes next."
I looked puzzled and asked, "What *does* come next?"
Grandma nodded towards the bucket, "We take our little friends for a walk," and then turning to her cat said, "and you can come too, I suppose!"
She produced a small leash and harness from her pocket and slipped it onto Dotty and off we set off up the lane at the side of Graymalkin Cottage. I held the leash and tried to keep pace with the cat while my grandmother carried the minibeasts. We stopped when the roof of the cottage was just visible in the distance and Grandma tipped the slimy contents of the bucket into a ditch at the side of the lane.
"Snails will come back to your garden unless you take them far enough away," she explained. After prodding one or two of the slugs that were heading for cover with her paw and finding them just as disgusting as I did, Dotty was eager to be off again and charged off down the path, while I struggled to hold on to her leash. We followed the track into the shady part of the lane where Grandma identified all

the small flowers in the hedgerows. I thought that their names sounded as unlikely as some of her sayings.

"Pennywort, Pimpernel, Toadflax and Catchfly," chanted Grandma in a singsong voice, while I, racing ahead with the wind in my hair called back as if completing a poem,

"And a cat called Dotty goes thundering by!"

As I lay in bed that night, I thought that staying at Graymalkin Cottage would not be too bad, after all.

Chapter 2

The next morning I was woken by the sound of rain on the roof slates above me and when I drew back the curtains, I was met by the sight of grey clouds, so low that they seemed to have covered the bottom of the field outside my window. Little rivulets of water ran down the path next to Graymalkin Cottage until they reached the end of the drive, where they formed an ever-growing puddle. Even with Grandad's binoculars, I would not have been able to see my house in this weather. I rested my chin on my hand, looked out at the darkening sky and knew that I would be bored today. I wished more than anything that I could be back in my own home with Ma.

"This weather is set in for the day," Grandma observed over breakfast. She looked at my gloomy face and added brightly, "....so, it's a cupboard day!" She went on to say that, as I was going to be staying for some time, it would be a good idea if we sorted out the cupboards in my room. That way, I could have my own space to organise as I wished and at the same time, she could get rid of some rubbish. I had always loved "cupboard days" at Grandma's. She never threw anything away and opening doors in every room always revealed shelves stacked high with Ma's and Aunt Hattie's old toys and books, photograph albums, dressing up costumes and collections of everything from thimbles to tea trays.

"One man's junk is another man's treasure," she said. I didn't ask, because for once I knew exactly what she meant. My room was larger than most in the house, because it formed the top floor of an extension my grandparents had added to the original cottage, as their family had grown many years before. Across the end wall, a row of eight doors reached from floor to ceiling. They had been built as wardrobes for my mother, as this had been her room when she was a child. Grandma opened the left hand door and took a deep breath, "Worse than I thought," she muttered. "This is going to take hours!" She tore three bin bags from a roll she had brought up from the kitchen and placed them on the floor in front of the cupboard. On three slips of paper, she wrote, "Keep", "Recycle/ Charity Shop" and "Bin" and placed one on each of the three bags. We began quite well, asking one another's advice if we were unsure about which pile something should go on, but then I would be distracted by a toy I wanted to play with or Grandma would find a book she wanted to read, and the sorting would come to a halt. However, after about two hours, three piles stood in front of us. The "Keep" pile was as least twice as high as the other two. Grandma shook her head, "The charity shops aren't going to do very well out of us!" I was eager to read some of the books I had found and thought the sooner we finished the other seven cupboards, the sooner I could start, so I rushed to the second door and pulled it open.

"Not that ..." Grandma did not have time to finish the sentence, before I found myself standing in front of a pile of slightly familiar objects.

"The boat!" I exclaimed.

It was not that she had managed to squeeze a twenty-eight foot yacht into a bedroom cupboard, but that everything that belonged on the yacht was in there or in one of the next three cupboards. Long narrow curtains, bright blue with a rope and anchor pattern, had been washed, pressed, neatly folded and stored in plastic bags. Beneath them the triangular cushions from the fore cabin stood behind the smaller ones from the bench seats. A box of charts, flags and books, together with the barometer, ship's clock and fog horn had been placed next to a large plastic tub labeled "Galley" from which saucepan handles and a wooden spoon protruded.

Grandad's pride and joy had been his boat, the *Fiona.* He used to joke that she was the only woman in his life apart from Grandma. When he was not sailing her, he would spend hours in the Old Harbour adding gadgets, fixing or, 'just plain tinkering', as Grandma would say.

"We last sailed just before the end of October," said Grandma wistfully. "We brought everything home to store in the dry, as we had done every year. You can't leave anything onboard during the winter. The cushions and curtains would be covered in mildew and charts and books don't like damp," She was finding it difficult to continue. Sighing, she said, "By

now, your Grandad would have been sailing every weekend."
"I'm sorry, Grandma," I said putting my arm round her. "I didn't mean to..."
"There's nothing to be sorry about," she said, then taking a deep breath, she sprang to her feet and said, "Right, I think it's time that we went to visit my old friend *Fiona!* If this rain eases off and tomorrow is fine, we'll take all of this over to the Old Harbour and make that boat ship shape and Bristol fashion!" I didn't ask what that meant, but was delighted at the prospect of seeing the boat again.
The next morning, I woke to the sunlight streaming through my curtains and was so excited by the thought of going to the Old Harbour, that I had showered and dressed before realising that it was only five-thirty in the morning. Trying not to make too much noise, I carefully opened the last "boat" cupboard and found Grandad's binoculars and a compass in a box marked 'Miscellaneous'. I tiptoed downstairs and quietly left the house by the back door. Placing the compass on the garden table, I waited for the needle to settle on north, then scanning the horizon, I looked, not for my house to the east, but for the Old Harbour to the northwest. A row of white masts came into focus and following them down to the water line, I spotted one with a light blue hull. Although I was unable to make out the name on her stern, in my mind's eye I saw the word, *Fiona,* written in black and gold lettering. I lowered the binoculars.

“I’ll look for my house tomorrow,” I told myself as I felt a soft, warm head nuzzling against my leg and a familiar chirp that meant, “Breakfast time!”.

Chapter 3

After breakfast, the contents of the boat cupboards were loaded into the Land Rover. We started by placing the large items, such as the cushions, in the boot area first. The second row of seats had been folded flat to make more room. I carried smaller objects, such as the kettle and sleeping bags downstairs and lined them up in the conservatory.
"They look like patients in a Waiting Room," I laughed.
"Mmmm," said Grandma, "waiting to see if there's room for them, no doubt." She struggled to lift some of the more awkward shaped pieces into the car, but after about half an hour, we had managed to fit everything in. Small items had been wedged between larger ones, pots and pans balanced on the top, while charts and books were posted under the seats.
"You'll have to hold the cat box on your lap," she said. "There's no room in the back."
She was almost at the door, keys in hand, when she turned back suddenly.
"I almost forgot," she said as she opened the door of the broom cupboard. Several spare leashes were hanging on a hook inside and next to them was a little, red life jacket with the words "SMALL DOG" printed on the side. An excited chirp from the pet carrier told me that it didn't belong to a dog, but to a very unusual cat.

With everything packed, we rattled along the lane from Graymalkin Cottage and slowly out onto the main road. Through the wing mirror, I could see a long line of impatient drivers behind us, eager to go about their day's business and annoyed that they had had the misfortune to get stuck behind someone who was driving only slightly faster than a snail's pace.

"They'll just have to wait," said Grandma, as every bend and corner caused the contents of the car to clatter and clank, slip and slide. After about ten minutes, we saw the sign for the Old Harbour and with one final lurch to the left, took the track down the lane towards the waterside. For about a mile, the lane ran parallel to a disused canal, at the end of which lay the inner basin. It was here that the *Fiona* had her berth and, as we approached I craned my neck to try to spot "the Old Girl", as Grandad used to call her.

"There she is!" I called out suddenly. "I can see her."

The Fiona was moored on the opposite bank, as the side nearest to the road had no proper pathway and any access there had been, had become overgrown with nettles and brambles long ago.

"Still afloat, then?" asked Grandma, with slightly less enthusiasm. She looked straight ahead, as if she was avoiding looking at the boat for as long as possible.

When we reached the car park next to the pontoon, she said, "Before we get out, we have got to deal with this flibberty-gibbet!" I didn't ask, but suspected that it was another one of her terms of endearment for her

cat. A harness and leash were produced from the glove box and slipped over Dotty's front legs.
"Now hold on to her," said Grandma. "Hold VERY, VERY tight!"
I soon understood the need for the warning, for as the door opened, Dotty shot out like an express train, straining at the leash and making her way towards the water's edge. I managed to pull her back and directed her towards the narrow crossing over the lock and up the cinder pathway on the other side. The lock separated the inner basin from the outer one, at the end of which stood a pair of massive lock gates and the Severn Estuary beyond. As we reached the top of the path, it turned to the right and ran along a narrow strip of land between the Severn to the left and the inner basin to the right. It seemed that the cat knew the way better than I did, because at a spot where the pathway became wider, she suddenly veered to the right and dragged me towards a small gate that was half hidden in the hedgerow. I lifted the makeshift rope loop that kept it shut and went down the stone steps on the other side. The pathway at the bottom passed several old boats that had been abandoned by their owners and I was glad that Grandma had decided to return to the *Fiona* and make her "ship-shape and Bristol fashion" rather than letting her rot away.
"Tie her onto one of the cleats on the stern," came a voice from behind me. Dotty leapt on to the *Fiona*'s deck in one bound, while I struggled to follow her on boar, untangling her leash from the guardrail as I did

so. Grandma was carrying the box of cleaning materials and was out of breath when she arrived. "Tightly!" she panted.
After a few attempts, my fingers remembered the rope pathways that Grandad had taught me and I executed a beautiful clove hitch that held the leash securely. The cat seemed to accept that she must sit patiently and was content to curl up on a neatly coiled rope at the back of the cockpit and watch through sly eyes, shoals of brown trout swimming by.
Although no-one had sailed or even visited the *Fiona* for many months, apart from a good covering of green algae on some parts of the deck, she looked clean and tidy. She was a French yacht with two cabins - a fore cabin and a saloon - separated by the Heads, which was the nautical name for the toilet. Her hull was blue and the name *Fiona* was picked out in black and gold lettering on her stern.
"Well," said Grandma, taking a deep breath, "I suppose we'd better get to work on this greenery, or people will sing 'The Owl and the Pussycat' as we go by!"
I looked puzzled for a moment and then laughing, realised what she meant and chanted, "The Owl and the Pussycat went to sea in a beautiful pea green boat!" Grandma joined in and together we recited the whole poem, adding the actions she had taught me when I was much younger. I would sit on her knee and we would share a picture book that illustrated the nonsense poem. I felt pleased that it was one of the

books that I had put in the "Keep" pile during our cupboard day.
"Hmm," mused Grandma, "if it's green on top, I think it will be grey below." She took a small key from her pocket and inserted it into the padlock that secured the hatch to the washboard. Grandad had explained that the entrance cover was named after the old-fashioned washboards that his mother would have scrubbed her clothes on, because it was similar in shape. The padlock opened easily and Grandma slid back the hatch and lifted the washboard onto the seat next to Dotty. She hesitated before going down into the cabin below and as if feeling the need to explain, turned to me and said, "Too many memories," and then cheerily added, "but most of them are good, so let's get on with it!" She nimbly climbed down the three wooden steps into the cabin and waited while I did the same.
"I'm glad we didn't leave anything on board," she said, running her finger over the grey mould that seemed to have covered every surface, "but we'll soon have her ..."
"Ship-shape and Bristol fashion!" I chimed in.
For the rest of the morning we cleaned and polished, sprayed and scrubbed. Grandma did the "nasty job", as she called it. This involved cleaning the Heads, but soon the little sea toilet looked brand new, the bright red wash basin gleamed and a clean towel had been hung on the hook behind the door. I cleaned the galley and, when all shelves were free from mold, I

thoroughly dried them so that the plates, mugs and dishes could be slotted into their racks.
Grandma opened the hatches in the fore cabin and saloon and said, "We'll let the air in and get everything nice and dry before we bring the cushions and curtains over." She filled the bucket with clean water, threw in two scrubbing brushes and said, "Time to swab the decks, me hearty!"
I started at the bow and Grandma at the stern and soon the white deck was returning to its former glory. It was just as I was moving from the port to the starboard side that I caught my foot on the latch on the anchor locker and would have fallen overboard if it had not been for making a last minute grab for the forestay. I held on tight, poised above the water and managed to swing myself back onto the deck.
"Land lubber!" The voice came from nearby and at first I could not see who had hurled the insult my way. A boy, about two or three years older than me, was paddling a small tender. As he drew level with our boat, I realised from the look of disgust on his face that he had made the statement.
"Bigheaded Boat Boy!" I retaliated, unable to think of a better insult at short notice. He was obviously so at home on the water that he would never fall overboard, or come anywhere close to it as I had done. He sat near the prow of the small boat rather than in the centre, the paddle dipping first to the left, then to the right. To show how superior he was, he totally ignored me and carried on to a large yacht moored in the middle of the basin.

“Lunch time!” Grandma called from the cockpit. I watched until the boy had tied the tender to the stern of the *Morning Star* and climbed on board, then made my way towards the stern.
“Goodness me!” Grandma exclaimed. “You look as if you’ve lost a bob and found a tanner!” I didn’t ask what that meant, but it sounded so funny that I forgot to be cross and smiled as I tucked into bread, cheese and lemonade. As we ate, I told her what had happened, giving more details about the Boat Boy and his rudeness than how I had almost fallen overboard and what I had said in return.
“He’s called Bob,” she said. “All three of us have not had the best of years and you two have got more in common than you might realise,” she said. “His father left home last year and his mother has had to go back to work full time. Every day, he comes over to their boat, starts the engine and just sits on her. If you watch him, he never looks out across the water, but instead sits facing the road. I think he hopes that one day his dad will drive down it and everything will be like it used to be.”
My father had left when I was a baby and had not been in touch since. I had never known him, so did not miss him ... but I missed Ma and I knew that Grandma missed Grandad. It was sometimes like an ache that could not be cured with medicines or with kind words and I felt sorry that I had not been more considerate towards Bob the Boat Boy.

Chapter 4

We cleared away the lunch scraps, tossing the last few breadcrumbs into the water, where they were quickly snapped up by the brown trout. As if on cue, Dotty woke up, stretched her legs and arched her back.

"All right, Missy," said Grandma,"I suppose you've earned it!" She rummaged in the box of dusters and produced the little, red life jacket with SMALL DOG printed on its side. At once the cat sprang into life, straining at her leash and chirping like a bird with a sore throat. Grandma held her on her lap, slipped the harness off, put the life jacket on and leaning over the boat's edge, gently lowered her into the water. Dotty set off across the basin, ears flattened to keep out the water and whiskers forward to warn her how close her nose was to its surface. Her front legs worked like tiny pistons and she chirped with excitement as she swam back and forth. She looked so funny that I clapped my hands and jumped up and down with excitement, laughing so loudly that people on the opposite bank left their picnic and moved closer to the water's edge to get a better look at what was going on. Mobile phones and cameras were produced and photographs and videos taken of the incredible swimming cat. Further up the basin, a man had been taking photographs of some of the old boats. He picked up his tripod and camera and hurried down to where the group was standing. He set up his equipment again, attaching a long lens to the camera and proceeding to take a series of shots.

"Keep an eye on her," said Grandma, "and tell me if she comes to the side of the boat." She was looking for something in the sail locker which went down as far as the bottom of the hull and I was torn between watching Dotty and watching Grandma in case she fell in among the lines and sails that were stored there.

I could see that the cat's leg movements were becoming less powerful and began to worry that she was starting to get tired.

"Grandma," I said, "I think she's coming over to the side of the boat. How do I get her out?" The waterline was too far down for me to reach her without falling in and I had already had one near miss today. Remembering my earlier slip, I looked over to the *Morning Star* and was surprised to see Boat Boy Bob watching the little cat's antics with a smile on his face.

At that moment, Grandma found what she had been looking for and getting to her feet, brandished a large net like the ones used by fishermen to keep their catch safe. With a loud swoosh, she swung it in a wide arc above her head and then deep down into the water, scooping Dotty up as she did and landing her unceremoniously on the deck. There was a round of applause and a few cheers from the people on the opposite bank, but I ignored them and was about to rush forward to disentangle the little cat from the net, when Grandma held me back.

“Give her a minute,” she said and I soon realised the reason for her caution, for as Dotty stood up, she shook herself vigorously, spraying everything in the cockpit with river water.

“I think I preferred lemonade!” observed Grandma, using one of the dusters to dry herself before wrapping the cat in a small towel which she had brought along for this purpose. She removed SMALL DOG and in less than five minutes, Dotty’s fur gleamed in the sunlight as she settled into her lengthy grooming routine.

“Excuse me!” We were startled by a voice from the path and I recognised the owner to be the photographer who had set up his tripod on the opposite bank a few minutes earlier. “Let me introduce myself,” he said holding out a small, white card. I think he could see from the way in which Grandma was holding the card at arm’s length and peering at it through narrowed eyes, that she was unable to read it without her glasses, so he added, “Clive Williamson, photographer for the *Clarion.”*

He held out his hand, which Grandma shook and asked, “And what can I do for you, Mr Williamson?”

“My newspaper is running a series of articles on the lesser known tourist attractions in the area and I was sent here today to take a few photographs of the Old Harbour and what goes on here. I must admit that I’ve spent weeks visiting places all over the County, but I’ve never quite seen anything like your cat. She’s the best tourist attraction I’ve ever seen. Just look at the crowd over there!”

The number of onlookers had increased and people were still looking toward the *Fiona* in the hope of seeing Dotty give a repeat performance. Those in the crowd, who had missed the event, were being shown videos of it on the mobile phones, taken by the people who had witnessed it first hand.

"She's not a circus act!" Grandma said indignantly. "She's just a cat that likes swimming. It's not uncommon in her breed."

Realising that he needed to continue with care, so as not to upset Grandma, he said, "She's one of the most beautiful cats I've ever seen." My grandmother smiled, feeling proud that in the matter of a few minutes Dotty had become a celebrity. "Would you consent to my taking a few more pictures of her?"

Grandma considered.

"With you two, of course," he added, sensing how protective of her cat Grandma felt, "and perhaps you wouldn't mind telling me a bit about her and how she came to become so fond of the water?"

As if she knew that she was the centre of attention, Dotty finished grooming and sat upright like the statue of the cat I had seen in the Egyptian department of the British Museum. Mr Williamson asked the two of us to sit, one either side of her and after Grandma had quickly combed her hair and applied a smudge of lipstick, he continued to take more photographs.

"Now, I'll need a few details," he said. "Few" was not a word Grandma used very often and she proceeded to give her name, my name, the cat's name and even the boat's name. When she started telling him about Dotty, I felt sorry for the poor man as he scribbled away, struggling to keep up with her account of how Bengal cats were first bred from the Asian Leopard Cat and how they had trained Dotty to be a boat cat and how she had shocked them by jumping into the water one day, and on and on and on....

"He'll have a book, not an article by the time she's finished!" I thought.

"Although she's a very good swimmer," continued Grandma, "cats can quickly become tired and drown. That's why we always put a life jacket on her. We tried several before finding one that was just right for her shape and size. Ironically, it was made for a ..."

"SMALL DOG," Mr Williamson seized the opportunity to get a word in by completing the sentence and so ending the interview. "Thank you Mrs Gates, Meg and, of course, Dotty," he said. "I'm going back to the office now and will put the article together. If my editor likes it, you should see something in the *Clarion* by Thursday."

"Thank you," said Grandma. "I've got your number, so I'll give you a ring if I think of anything we haven't covered."

Mr Williamson was already hurrying along the path, but called back over his shoulder, "Don't worry, Mrs Gates, I'm sure that I've got more than enough information for the article!"

"More than enough to fill ten newspapers," I thought.

Chapter 5

"Is that the time?" Grandma looked at her watch. "It's past two o'clock and we've still got lots to do before we can go home, so shake a leg!" I didn't ask!

If we could have swam backwards and forwards, to and from the car park, the task of unloading everything and bringing it to the boat would have been an easy one, but our route over land took us along the overgrown path at the side of the *Fiona,* up a flight of stone steps with a rickety hand rail, along the cinder track between the inner basin and the Severn, across the lock and through a gate to the car park. After our second journey from car to boat, laden with cushions and curtains, Grandma declared herself to be, "Fair tuckered", and although I didn't ask, I think I understood what she meant. We finished putting the small bench cushions in place in the saloon, hung the curtains at the narrow windows and were about to set off again when we heard a strange noise on the pathway. We both stood still and listened as it got closer and closer. I thought that it sounded like a someone blowing a toy trumpet in a rhythmic, monotonous way.

"Sounds like broken bellows, and that can only be ..." and popping her head through the companion way hatch, called out, "....Billy O!"

"Heave to and prepare to be boarded!" came the reply, followed by a long wheeze.

"How are you, you salty old sea dog?" asked Grandma, as an elderly man with white whiskers and a Breton cap climbed aboard and hugged her.

"Oh dear," I thought, "he must have caught strange sayings from Grandma ... or perhaps she caught them from him!" I knew that I would need to concentrate really hard if I had any chance of understanding a word that either of them was saying.

"I'm afraid to say I'm bilged on my anchor. I daresay I'll be crossing the bar before long!" he said with a tinge of sadness in his voice. Grandma later explained that Billy O had been a great sailor in his youth - fit, strong and fearless - but he had developed a lung disease that could not be cured. He didn't like to admit that he was ill, so he used nautical terms to avoid having to talk about it.

Noticing me, he gave one loud wheeze and said cheerily, "Is this your galley slave?"

Grandma laughed and made the introductions, "Meg, this is Captain William O'Donnell, better known as Billy O; Billy O, this is my granddaughter, Megan."

He removed his cap and bent low to kiss my hand, adding, "Any granddaughter of the late Captain Gates, God rest his soul, is a granddaughter of mine!" He winked and I was unsure how to reply, so I just smiled and thanked him.

"Now," he said, "I've not left my Watch and dragged my old carcass across here for nothing." I later found out that his "Watch" involved sitting in a battered, old,

deck chair from morning to late evening, looking out down the river to the Bristol Channel beyond. "That car of yours is loaded to the gunwales," he continued, "and you'll be here until midnight if you mean to carry everything along the path ... unless you don't collapse first!"
"Don't think you're going to help us," warned Grandma.
"Ah,' he replied, "there's more than one way to skin a cat!" Turning to me, he said, "Gran'daughter, do you know how to cast off?"
"Aye, aye, Captain!" I replied and he gave a deep chuckle, which set off a fit of wheezing and coughing.
"The engine hasn't been started for months and..." Grandma started to look for excuses, but he silenced her protests with,
"None of yer blathering," and then gave a command, as if he was the captain of a great sailing vessel, "Fire her up!"
She knew that it was pointless to argue, so Grandma removed the engine cover and turned a small knob to open the seacocks and after she had replaced it, flicked the power switch. She was reassured by the appearance of a row of lights on the control panel. Pressing the starter button resulted in a few whirs and wheezes that reminded me of Billy O, until suddenly, the engine roared into life. Perhaps "roared" is an exaggeration, as it sounded more like a cross between a lawnmower and an old tractor, but at least it was running.

"I don't think you ought to ..." Grandma started to say, concerned that the old man would not manage to negotiate even the short journey from berth to pontoon.
"I'm not going to," he replied. "*You* are!"
It was well understood by anyone who knew her that Grandma did not like taking the helm. When she and Grandad had sailed, he had always taken the tiller and she had been the navigator. She had been in charge of plotting their course on the charts, keeping an eye out for hazards and watching the depth gauge. Before she could make any further protests, Billy O had started to give his instructions. On his signal, I was to "slip the lines" and jump back on board; Grandma was to check the fenders and then take the tiller and he was to sit in the cockpit and give advice. His advice seemed to consist of calling out, "for'ard", "astern", "port" and "starboard" and as we manoeuvred out of the berth and into the main basin, these commands came thick and fast. With care rather than skill, Grandma managed to steer a course towards the pontoon and as we approached, a new set of commands were issued. Some of these were aimed at me and involved making the lines ready to tie up when we arrived. Billy O showed me how to hold the lines so that I would be able to jump off and "make us fast", as he called it, as quickly as possible. Luckily, when we arrived at the pontoon, it was empty of other boats and so our mooring was easy. I could see that Grandma was relieved to have arrived

safely, but she was also proud that she had achieved a "first", as she called it later.
"My home port, I think," said Billy O. "You're welcome to come and visit me on my Watch, young Gran'daughter." With another cough and a very loud wheeze, he stepped onto the pontoon and made his way slowly and stiffly back to his old deck chair. We listened to his progress which was marked with more rasps and wheezes and several pauses, until a look of panic suddenly came across Grandma's face and she called after him,
"How do we get the *Fiona* BACK to her berth?"
"Well," he said slowly, "you could always get that cat of yours to tow you over." This was followed by a fit of laughter that sounded more like a whistling kettle, then with a cackle and a hiss he added, " You're more than capable of doing it."
She shouted, "Marooned by my own captain!"
This was met by more coughing and wheezing, and then finally with a deep breath he called out, "Fair winds and following seas!" I didn't ask, but I was beginning to realise that I would never understand what they were talking about unless I did ask, so decided to start questioning their strange sayings.
Billy O had been right when he had suggested loading the boat from the pontoon, as the car was a short distance away and there were only two small steps to carry things down. In next to no time we had put all the remaining cushions in place and the galley had been equipped with a wide-bottomed whistling kettle, frying pan and an assortment of knives, forks,

spoons and a large ladle for serving Grandma's speciality, Ship's Stew. Charts were placed neatly in their drawer and books with titles like, "Know Your Knots", "Reading the Clouds" and "Safe Harbours of the South" were lined up on the shelf next to the control panel. She stood and looked at the cabins and smiled a satisfied smile. I waited for her to say, "Ship-shape and Bristol fashion", so that I could ask EXACTLY what it meant, but she did not. Instead, she went up into the cockpit. I think it might have been an attempt to delay having to take the *Fiona* back across the basin on her own, but she decided that the Red Ensign and a set of special pennants were missing and set about searching for them in the sail locker.

"If she doesn't say anything strange, how can I ask her what it means?" I thought. And then I had an idea. A few weeks before, I had heard her talking to Aunt Hattie and she had said something very odd, even for her.

"Grandma," I said.

An indistinct, "Yes, dear" came from the sail locker.

"Where is the 'Town of Tribulation'?"

"Town of Tribulation?" the muffled voice questioned. "There's no such place."

"But I heard you and Aunt Hattie talking about it a few weeks ago and I wondered where it is."

She continued to explore the depths of the locker in her search for the missing flags, but said again, "There's no such place. You must have been mistaken."

I was determined to learn the meaning of at least one strange saying, so I pressed the point with, “You said to Aunt Hattie that you had passed the 'Town of Tribulation'. I know I heard you say it.”
There was a moment’s silence and at first I thought that she was angry with me, then from the locker a small sound was heard. It started as a stifled snigger, then it grew until it had erupted into a great belly laugh and Grandma abandoned her search and leapt up, cutting through the air with the flag pole, as if it was a pirate’s cutlass.
“Past the Town of Tribulation and Straight on to Derring Do!” she shouted, as I looked on in amazement. She laughed so much that tears streamed down her cheeks, until finally she sat down heavily on the cockpit seat and explained, “ What I actually said was that I had passed through many ‘trials and tribulations’, not the 'Town of Tribulation'. It means that I had problems, but they were over at last.”
I smiled and nodded, “I’m sorry, I must have misheard,” but feeling that my understanding of strange sayings still needed to improve, I added, “ and by the way, where is Derring Do?”
My question seemed to start another fit of laughing and waving of the “cutlass”, but finally she admitted, “You know, I haven’t got a clue ... but it sounds like the sort of place where you can have adventures.” We both laughed and then, just as Billy O had done, she started to give her instructions,

"Make ready to slip the lines," she said. "Nobody ever had an adventure while they were tied to a pontoon!"

I was proud of the way she took the small boat back across the basin and how we worked together to make sure that the *Fiona* was moored securely when we reached the other side. I looked across to the *Morning Star* in the hope that Boat Boy Bob had seen how successfully we had managed the boat, but his father's yacht was closed up and the fact that the tender was back near the pontoon told us that he had obviously gone home.

Grandma closed the cabins and was about to turn the key in the padlock when she remembered something. Going down into the saloon again, she opened her bag and produced a framed photograph neatly wrapped in newspaper. After unpeeling the layers, she took a tissue out of her pocket and breathed on the glass, giving it a polish before hanging it on a hook next to the barometer. It was a photograph of Grandad at the tiller. A small brass label had been screwed onto the bottom edge of the frame and in an old fashioned script the words on it said,

"Captain Andrew Gates of the Good Ship *Fiona*"

Grandma smiled and gave it a final polish before closing the cabin again.

Chapter 6

As with most summers, one fine day was followed by a downpour and having spent Tuesday morning finding places for my belongings in the now empty cupboards, I did not look forward to an afternoon with nothing to do. After lunch, sensing that I was bored, Grandma produced a leather-bound book from the shelf above the computer and asked if I would like to look at it. She explained that all good sailors keep a log of their activities. As navigator, it had been her job to record details of each journey, together with facts about wind, weather and tides. Before opening it, I used my finger to trace the faded gold lettering on the worn cover that told me that this was the log of the *Fiona.* Instead of the boring lists and tables that I had expected to see between its covers, I was surprised to find the little book fascinating. The first pages were dated long before I was born and told of my grandparents' first unsteady steps into sailing. Sometimes they had run aground and on one occasion had to be towed off a sandbank by a friend. Twice, they recorded having received Mayday calls from other boats, helping in a rescue from one of them. The later entries would often be accompanied by photographs or small, line-drawn maps that had been stuck to the back of each page. The last few were special because they included Dotty, usually

sitting on her coiled rope mat and wearing SMALL DOG.
"Why don't you start a log?" suggested Grandma.
"But we don't sail anywhere," I said sadly, wishing more than anything that we could go out of those huge lock gates at the entrance to the Old Harbour and under the pair of bridges I could see from the pier head, down the Bristol Channel and out towards the open sea. In my mind's eye, I would visit Lundy Island and find a pirate's cave, then further down the Channel, we would round St. David's Head, while dolphins played alongside in Ceredigion Bay.
My day dream was interrupted by Grandma's laugh, "We sailed yesterday. I know it wasn't far, but it was ... interesting!" she said. "Anyway your log could be a record of everything you do while you're staying here. That way, when you see your mother you'll not forget to tell her about any of your adventures."
I gave her a faint smile but feeling that I would have no adventures to tell her about said, "I just wish we could sail somewhere."
She laughed, "If wishes were horses, beggars would ride!" I was starting to understand some of her sayings. I had worked out that the best of them conjured up a picture of an idea. However, in my picture the wishes were boats and the beggars were sailing!
She had produced a small ring-bound note book and after tearing out the first few pages on which she had written shopping lists, wrote on the first clean page,

"Past the Town of Tribulation and Straight on to Derring Do" by Megan Waterfield.
I sat and stared at the blank page, unsure how to begin, then a picture of Boat Boy Bob and the Swimming Cat crept into my mind, so I started with a drawing both of them. By the end of the afternoon, I had filled six pages with words and pictures before closing the book and placing it on the shelf above my bed.
"Tomorrow's weather is looking good," Grandma said as we were eating our evening meal. "I have to wait for Mr Sykes, the builder to come and fix that down pipe outside the kitchen door. He should have finished by lunchtime, so we'll go over to the Old Harbour when he's gone."
It was about 1 o'clock when we arrived at the car park the next day. It was so full that we had difficulty in finding somewhere to park.
"Busy for a Wednesday," Grandma said. "The fine weather must have brought them all out." She slipped the harness and leash onto Dotty and handed it to me, while she went to the back of the car to collect SMALL DOG and a box of biscuits she had baked for Billy O.
As I got out, a woman in the next car opened her door and cried excitedly,
"It's HER, it's the Salty Sea Cat!" At the same time, a small Jack Russell terrier leapt off her lap and started to snap at my heels. As I was trying to fend off the dog, I let go of the leash and Dotty, thinking that she

was under attack, raced off straight towards the dockside.
"STOP!" I cried out, but Dotty felt that she would be safer in the water, so that was exactly where she was heading. I saw Grandma standing at the back of the car with SMALL DOG in her hands and a look of desperation on her face.
"Oh, no," I thought, "she'll drown!" I knew that the water in the outer basin was very deep and that there was a drop of at least ten feet before you reached it. I called out to a group of people standing near the edge, "Stop that cat!", but my voice was carried away on the wind.
It was then that the most amazing thing happened. From out of nowhere, Boat Boy Bob raced up and threw himself across the panicking animal's path, just as if he was a goalkeeper making a save. I often replay that scene in my mind and it appears that he lunged at her in slow motion, hitting the floor with a thud and reaching out for the passing cat. Unfortunately, she was so nimble that she zigzagged around him and had passed him before he hit the floor. With one last frantic effort, he shot out his arm and managed to hold onto the end of the leash, just as Dotty went over the edge of the dock. We heard a loud chirp, as the harness brought her to a juddering halt and she was left hanging in mid air against the wall of the outer basin. By the time I reached them, Bob had hauled her up onto the dockside and was cradling her in his arms. She seemed to be calmed

by the soothing way he was speaking and he carried on stroking her gently.
Tears were rolling down my cheeks and it was all that I could do to blurt out, “Thank you!” Boat Boy Bob told me later that I said it about twenty times between sobs. By this time, Grandma had come across to us, accompanied by the woman whose dog had caused Dotty to set off at such a speed. I was pleased to see that the dog was now shut in her car, although his pacing backwards and forwards showed how anxious he was to join us.
At first I thought I would be in trouble for letting go of the leash, but Grandma was more interested in showing me the newspaper that the lady had given her.
“I was shopping in town,” explained the woman, “and picked up a copy of the lunchtime edition of the *Clarion.* I was flicking through it when I found the article on the Salty Sea Cat and just had to come and see her for myself. I’m so sorry that my naughty Arthur frightened your cat. He loves cats!”
“Mmm,” said Grandma, “but I bet he couldn’t eat a whole one!” It was such a silly thing to say, but it was just what was needed to stop everyone being upset and soon we were all laughing. This was the second time that I had seen Boat Boy Bob smile. The woman with the Jack Russell felt guilty about causing such distress to the little cat, not to mention to Grandma and myself, so she left us with her copy of the *Clarion* saying she would get another one on the way home.

As I held the leash tightly, we all sat down on the grass and turned to page five.
"Wow," said Bob, " she's a super star! No wonder all these people are here. Look they've got their cameras ready to take photographs."
"Well, they will just have to wait until her ladyship is properly dressed!"
Grandma read the article out loud to us. It was headed, "Salty Sea Cat" and told how this special little cat had her own life jacket and loved to do the "catty paddle" across the inner basin. There was no mention of any of the attractions of the Old Harbour, except for the little Bengal cat who loved to swim there. Grandma would break in to her reading by saying things like, "Look at my hair in that photograph. What a fright!" and, "I'm glad he mentioned about the Asian Leopard Cat" and so many more interruptions that I thought we would never get to the end. As she finished, we all declared it to be the best article we had ever read and felt extremely proud to know such an unusual cat.
"Right madam," she addressed the remark to Dotty. "Showtime!". SMALL DOG was strapped securely around the little cat's body and she was carried over the lock, up the cinder path, through the gate and down the steps to the *Fiona.* A cheer went up from the crowd as Grandma lowered her into the water. I set about opening the sail locker, so that the net would be ready as soon as she started to grow tired. It was as if she knew that she had an audience of admirers, because she swam for much longer and

ventured closer to the far bank than on the previous occasion. When Grandma finally scooped her out of the water with a flourish that made her look like a ringmaster at the circus, the crowd applauded and cheered.

"Now you two," she said to Bob and I, "dry her off and tie her to the cleat. I won't be long." She handed us the tin of biscuits, winking at Bob and adding that at least one of us had deserved a treat and that she would make another batch for Billy O tomorrow.

We watched as several members of the crowd approached Grandma on the way back to the car and realised that they were asking her to sign their copies of the article. Finally, she was able to drive off, returning a few minutes later with an arm full of newspapers.

"Well," she said, "there's one for your mum, one for Bob's mum, one for Aunt Hattie ..." the list was endless, but finally she added, "and one for your log."

That evening I sat and completed the day's entry, sticking the article onto the back of the page. As I wrote about our adventure, I looked forward to my next visit to the Old Harbour and the new friend I had made. When Grandma came in to say goodnight, she said that she was pleased that Bob and I were now getting on well.

"After all," she said, "it's not first impressions that count as much as last ones!" And I think I understood what she meant.

Chapter 7

When we arrived at the Old Harbour on Thursday morning, I was disappointed to see that the *Morning Star* was deserted and her tender was still tied to the pontoon. I also had a secret worry that now everything was in its place on board the *Fiona,* Grandma would feel that we would not need to visit as frequently as we had been doing. However, I think that she was enjoying Dotty's fame and felt obliged to put on a show for the people who came to watch the little cat swimming every day. When Dotty was not performing for her audience, Grandma seemed content to sit and read in the sunshine or to cook bacon sandwiches in the galley. Although she would start the engine each day, she made no further attempts to sail anywhere and my dreams of adventures on the high seas were disappearing. I had just begun to practice some of the trickier exercises found in 'Know your Knots', when Boat Boy Bob's head appeared above the side of the *Fiona.*

"Is it okay if the Land Lubber comes up the canal?" He addressed his question to my grandmother, but knew that I would be the one who answered.

"Oh, Grandma PLEASE," I begged, expecting a lecture about safety and staying where she could see me. Instead she encouraged me to go and advised Bob to tie up further along the path where a metal

ladder that ran from the path down to water level, would make it easier for me to get into the small rowing boat.
"Life jacket!" she called after me as I was about to climb onto the path. When she was satisfied that buckles and straps were sufficiently tight, I made my way to the top of the ladder. I had seen Boat Boy Bob kneeling at the bow and paddling his small boat effortlessly, as if it was a canoe and he was Hiawatha. Because he did it with such ease, it had never occurred to me that even getting on board was far harder than it appeared. Looking down from the top of the ladder, I realised that I did not know how to begin. Much to his amusement, I was about to find out. He kept the boat as steady as he could by holding on to the metal ladder, while I wobbled and and teetered and tried very hard not to fall overboard.
"Stay in the centre and keep as low as you can," Bob said, with a mixture of panic and amusement in his voice. Finally I managed to stop swaying like a seesaw and sat down heavily on the plank seat.
"Land lubber!" he teased trying to hide his laughter as I held tightly to the sides of the boat.
We set off up the inner basin, past a rusting trawler and a clinker-built schooner and past the rowing club's skiff. When we had almost reached the swing bridge at the far end, we came alongside a large, white motor yacht. It stood out against some of the ramshackle, abandoned boats around it, because it was much newer and much more expensive. The name *Dans Vers* was painted on the stern.

As we approached, a woman appeared on deck and shouted, "Keep your distance, teenage nuisances!" I was shocked by her rudeness as we were nowhere near her boat and I was nowhere near being a teenager.

Bob carried on rowing calmly, but when we had passed under the swing bridge, he shook his head and said, "Miss Danvers is the most horrible person I know. She's mean to everybody around her and thinks she owns the place."

"You used to think I was the most horrible person you knew," I laughed and Bob gave the paddle a little flick and splashed me with water. I was feeling much braver now and managed to let go of the side with one hand, dip it in the water and return the favour. We both laughed and I let out a loud squeal as the small boat rocked.

This had the effect of bringing Miss Danvers on deck again and before disappearing below she shouted, "Hooligans!", in our direction. I covered my mouth to avoid bursting into laughter and Bob rowed away at speed.

"That's not a proper boat anyway," he muttered. "It hasn't got sails!"

I forgot about Miss Danvers, as soon as we passed under the bridge and into the disused canal. The bank on the left was steep with a path running along the top that was used mainly by dog walkers and visitors, because it had the best view of the River Severn for miles around. However, from our place in the boat, it seemed that we were in a steep-sided canyon with the bank on the left and tall reeds on the right. The water had a strange stillness to it, Bob's paddle hardly making a ripple on its surface. Below us, the water weed swayed gently backwards and forwards and the only sound was a gentle rustling of the wind in the long grasses.

A shout, loud and unexpected startled me so that I caused the boat to rock again.

"Yo, Bob," a voice from the top path hailed us. "Is that your girlfriend?"

Bob shaded his eyes with one hand and was able to make out two familiar figures against the skyline.

"No, it's my little sister," he answered.

"Hello Bob's sister," said one of the boys. I raised a hand in a sort of small wave and without any further comment the two boys disappeared out of view, down the other side of the top path towards the rocks and wrecked boats on the shoreline.

"Sorry about that," said Bob when they had gone. "That was Phil Renney and Dave Higgins from my class. They're okay, but can be tricky if you don't handle them properly." I could see that he obviously knew how to do that by not giving them the chance to tease or bully him about a girlfriend.

" I haven't seen them here since the Easter holidays," he continued. "They got onto one of the abandoned boats and Miss Danvers called the police. They weren't doing anything wrong, but the police told them that they were trespassing and went to see their parents. Phil's dad couldn't have cared less, but Dave was grounded for a week. "The Danvers" is not their favourite person." I decided there and then, that I would avoid Miss Danvers whenever possible.

A few hundred metres along the canal, we were confronted by a wall of tall, slender-leaved reeds and the water weed had become so thick that Bob seemed to scoop great clumps of it up with each stroke of the oar.

"Time to turn back," he said, explaining that all the canal was like this until a few years ago, when money had been given to the Old Harbour so that part of it could be cleared.

"There's not much more of the canal. It finishes about half a mile further on," he said. "It was built to link up with the railway when the Old Harbour was busy with all sorts of boats."

Using the paddle on one side, he turned the boat in a semi circle. Our voices must have disturbed a swan, whose nest was somewhere in the dense reeds ahead and it reared up, wings outstretched and charged towards us.

"Cripes!" said Bob and paddled furiously. I looked back and saw that the magnificent bird, having defended its territory, had gone back to its nest, It was more eager to protect its young than to catch us.

Passing under the swing bridge, he gave "The Danvers" a wide berth, because as he said, "We've been shouted at enough for one day!"

Instead of taking me straight back to the *Fiona,* he tied up to the stern of the *Morning Star* and helped me onto the low bathing platform. As we climbed the ladder on her stern, I felt honoured that Bob had invited me onto his father's boat, because I knew that it was his special place. With great pride, he gave me a tour of the boat, pointing out some of the things his father had added. The *Morning Star* was much larger than the *Fiona* and being a modern boat had things that the "Old Girl" did not have. Down below, there were three large cabins and a galley that had a fridge and a full size cooker. The heads had hot water and a shower and in the saloon there was a TV on the wall. On deck, there were solar panels and a wind vane to generate electricity, a lazy jack to make hoisting the mainsail easier and a life raft was secured to the pushpit at the stern. It soon became obvious how Bob spent his time on board, as each line was hanging, neatly coiled in a figure of eight. Even in the sail locker, spare lines hung from their hooks and sail bags were smartly lined up in order of size. I could not help thinking how different our boat was and how Grandma was always in danger of getting lost in the clutter of our sail locker.

When I said as much, Bob looked at me sadly and said, "But your boat is loved; mine has been deserted."

I could see that he was thinking about his father and how he had deserted not only his boat, but also his family.

"Did your dad run far?" I asked. "Mine ran off when I was born and didn't stop running until he got to Australia. Grandma always calls him 'Derek the Departed'."

"No," he said quietly. "Only as far as Somerset. I'm going to see him this weekend, but ... " His voice trailed away and he stretched out on the bench seat in the cockpit. I lay back on the seat on the other side and for a few minutes, we said nothing as we watched small white clouds drifting across the deep, blue sky. Suddenly, I remembered how I used to spend lazy afternoons with Ma, lying on the grass and finding animals and faces in the clouds above us. I pointed to a pair of small wedge shaped clouds floating above us.

"Look," I said, "there's the *Fiona,* closely followed by *Morning Star* !"

"And I suppose that dark one over there is 'The Danvers'!"

We both laughed and for a moment, Bob forgot to be sad. A voice from the other side of the harbour called out,

"Time to go!"

"I won't be here tomorrow. I'm going to see Ma," I told him as we made our way back to the metal ladder alongside the *Fiona.*

"See you on Monday, then," he said and I watched as he took the tender over to the pontoon, then collecting his bicycle, he set off along the road alongside the canal towards home.

That evening, I completed my log by adding details of everything that had happened that day. I drew a map of the Old Harbour, showing the mooring places of the *Fiona,* the *Morning Star* and the *Dans Vers.* I sketched the swing bridge and the canal beyond it, including the path where Bob's classmates had been walking and showing how it led down to the rocks and the bank of the River Severn. On the opposite side of the canal, I drew the road that we travelled along to get to the Old Harbour. Finally, I marked the swan's nest in a shaded area that showed where the reeds were too thick to allow boats to go any further. I wrote about my first trip in a rowing boat and how I had almost tipped it over. I described my meeting with 'The Danvers' and added a drawing of her sour face with a speech bubble that contained the words, "I hate teenagers!". I included a description of the *Morning Star* and how Bob looked after her. I did not mention how his father had run away, because I knew that Ma would read it and it might remind her of when my father had left and make her sad.

The following day, she sat and read it from cover to cover while Grandma and Aunt Hattie prepared our lunch. She asked me questions about the people I had met and smiled weakly when I told her about how Dotty had become famous and how many people came to watch her swim. I noticed that Ma ate very little, pushing most of her food into a pile at the edge of the plate, so that it would appear that she had eaten more than she had. It is the same trick that I use if I don't like something. After lunch, Aunt Hattie said that it was time for Ma to have a nap and so we kissed her goodbye and set off back to Graymalkin Cottage.

I sat in silence for the first part of the journey. I had been so busy with everything that had happened at the Old Harbour, that I had not given much thought to anything else and now I felt selfish. Finally, I had to ask,

"Ma is very ill, isn't she Grandma?"

"No, Meg," she replied. "She has BEEN very ill. Now she's going to get better ... but we have to be patient. It will take time."

Chapter 8

The first thing we saw when we arrived at the Old Harbour on Monday morning, was a police car parked near to the pontoon. As we unloaded our car and attached Dotty's leash to her harness, we looked down to the place where Boat Boy Bob kept his tender and could see a police officer, standing next to him with a notebook in his hand. Every so often he would write something in it before asking Bob further questions. I scanned the rest of the harbour and could see that another police officer was talking to Billy O at the end of the pier and a third was walking along the tow path, prodding and poking the bushes with a long pole.

"What's going on here then?" said Grandma.

We did not have to wait long before we found out, because the policeman who had been talking to Bob seemed to have finished his interview and now turned his attention on us.

"Excuse me, madam," he called out to Grandma. "Do you have a boat here?"

She said that she did and pointed to the *Fiona* on the other side of the dock. He asked if she would mind going over to the boat with him, to check that all was in order. He explained that some boats had been broken into during the weekend and equipment had been stolen. Grandma looked anxious, so I allowed Dotty to set off along the cinder path at top speed, while I held onto her leash. I wanted to get to the boat before anyone else arrived in case it had been damaged, and a runaway cat was a good excuse. To my great relief everything on board was just as we had left it. When Grandma and the policeman arrived, he had a look around and, satisfied that nothing was amiss, was about to retrace his steps along the path, when Boat Boy Bob called to him from the *Morning Star,*

"Everything is okay here!"

I was not aware of Miss Danvers' approach until a voice at the side of the boat said frostily,

"Well, it would be, wouldn't it? They don't steal from one another, do they?"

Ma had always told me to speak to grown ups with respect, but I felt my arms become rigid at my sides, my fists clench and a red mist swirl round my brain. I could not help myself.

"How can you be so mean to Bob! He's the kindest, most honest, most helpful, most ..." Here I ran out of 'mosts', so I drew a deep breath and blurted out, " Anyway, he wasn't even here this weekend. He was staying with his dad in Somerset."

The police officer, as grown ups often do, did not want to take a child's word for it and looked to my grandmother for confirmation.

"Is that true?"

"Yes," she said. "My granddaughter doesn't tell lies!"

The Danvers huffed and said, "Well, if it wasn't him, it was probably those friends of his!" and wagging her finger at the policeman, added," Go and check your

records and you'll see that they've been in trouble before. Teenage troublemakers!"
She was keen to change the subject rather than to apologise, so she handed him a piece of paper. "I've made an inventory of everything that has been stolen from the *Dans Vers,*" she said.
He scanned the list, and pointed to the last two items.
"A ship's brass barometer with a square of blue paint on the back," he read out.
"The blue paint was a result of my father hanging it on the wall in the hallway before the paint had dried," she explained.
"Old style binoculars with brass eyepieces, engraved on the side with, 'Presented to Cpt. E. Danvers 1947'," he continued.
"My father's, obviously," she added.
"The electrical items will be hard to trace, but these two are quite distinctive." They had started to walk along the path that led towards the *Dans Vers,* so the rest of their conversation was lost.
Grandma turned to me and said, "Phew, you certainly got your steam up!" and raising one hand in the air, tugged on an invisible cord and made a sound like an old locomotive. "Toot, Toot!"
I felt my arms relax and the beginnings of a smile creep into the corners of my mouth.
"She certainly got your dander up!" she continued.
"More like my "Danvers" up," I giggled and we both began to laugh so loudly that the lady in question

turned and gave us her usual sour glare, as we stifled our giggles and ducked below into the cabin.
Boat Boy Bob announced his arrival with a bang on the side of the boat as he secured the tender to the *Fiona's* stern. It startled the little cat who, despite all the commotion, was asleep on her coiled rope and she gave a loud chirp.
"Permission to come aboard," he called out, as he clambered into the cockpit.
"Well, it seems that he thinks it's better to ask for forgiveness than permission," said Grandma. I did not ask, as I was beginning to understand more and more of her sayings.
"I was waiting for her to go," he said nodding in the direction of The Danvers.
"She's horrible," I said to Bob. "She thinks you're in car boots with those boys from school."
There was a moments silence, as Bob and Grandma exchanged puzzled glances, then at the same time, worked out what I meant.
"Cahoots," said Grandma. "You mean, she thinks you're in cahoots with them ... and don't ask me what it means, because I haven't got a clue!" This was the cause of so much laughter that Grandma took out a small handkerchief and wiped the tears from her eyes. When we had calmed down again, she said,"Actually, you might have an idea there. The thieves will try to get rid of what they've stolen very quickly, so I think we ought to keep our eyes open at the car boot sale in the market square on Saturday."

Bob and I nodded, but both of us would rather be sailing than shopping.
A little while later, as he rowed towards the canal, he told me about his weekend. His father and his new girlfriend had taken him to an air show, followed by dinner at a restaurant overlooking the local marina.
" 'Call me Mel', she kept saying. She was trying to get me to like her, but it was obvious that I didn't like her and she didn't like me," he said. "I told Dad I didn't want to visit him again if "Call-me-Mel" was going to be there and he got angry and brought me home early."
We passed under the swing bridge, taking care to give The Danvers a wide berth and continued slowly up the canal. As we drew near to the thick reeds where the swan had its nest, Bob said that we had better turn early, to avoid disturbing the bird again. At that point, the reeds on either side were so thick and dense that it was difficult to make a complete circle, and we ploughed into a large clump near the roadside bank. As the tall stems parted, I caught a glimpse of something in the shallow water near to the edge. At that moment, the sun came from behind a cloud and caused the water to sparkle, bright and golden around the object.
"Look," I called to Bob, "there's something in the water over there!"
He tried to beat down the undergrowth with the oar, but we were too far away to reach. He moved as far forward in the boat as he could and was about to try to take hold of the object when I pulled him back.

“Wait,” I said, “ that looks like a pair of brass binoculars.” I suspected that this was the pair that had been stolen from The Danvers and if we went back with them, she would accuse Bob of taking them.

He considered for a moment and then said, “You’re right. We’d better get your Grandma.” He rowed back as quickly as he could, not even bothering to avoid passing close to the *Dans Vers.* Luckily, her owner was nowhere to be seen and we were soon in sight of the *Fiona.*

Grandma was sitting on deck and after we had gabbled out our discovery, she stood up and called across to the car park, where the three policemen were loading their car ready to leave. She told them to wait there, while she walked round by the pathway, instructing us to row back to the place where we had seen the binoculars and wait while she came along the road with the police officers.

“You’ll know the spot,” said Bob. “I could see the big oak tree in the lane when the reeds flattened.” He told Grandma that the oak tree stood near to a passing place on the lane, so they should be able to park there.

A few minutes later we listened as the police car drew up and a voice called out to us,

“Is this the place?”

Bob waved the oar in the air, so that it would be seen from the bank.

Right,” the voice commanded. “P. C. Raines, wellingtons, if you please!”

"Yes, Sarge," came the less than enthusiastic reply. Through the curtain of reeds, we could just recognise the young policeman who had spoken to us earlier, make his way to the waters edge wearing a pair of wellingtons that finished well below his knee. We could hear him muttering and mumbling as the slimy, green water flowed over the top of them and soaked his socks.
"Got them, Sarge!" he called out, brandishing the binoculars so vigorously above his head, that he lost his balance and sat down heavily, with a splash among the reeds. This activity sent a wave towards our boat and caused it to rock so violently that I thought we would end up in the water with him.
The sergeant showed little sympathy for him, calling out, "Mind the evidence!" Shaking his head he added, "P. C. Raines: Wet by name and wet by nature!" He ordered the third policeman to fetch the pole, which was eventually extended towards the floundering police constable.
"Not you!" shouted the sergeant as the young man made a grab for it. "Hook the binoculars onto it." and turning to Grandma, he explained that the evidence must be preserved at all costs. Grandma doubted that P. C. Raines would have shared that view. Once the binoculars had been carefully placed in a large, plastic bag, the pole was offered once more and a very wet policeman was hauled back onto dry land. We were about to turn back towards the pontoon when I heard Grandma say,
"What's that at the edge of the reeds?"

"Looks like an old carrier bag to me. Probably blown in by the wind," said P. C. Raines, reluctant to go anywhere near to the water again. He was relieved when Bob, who had managed to steady the boat, called back, "It's okay. I can reach it with the oar."

We dragged it onboard and after the water had drained out of a hole in the bottom, declared it to be empty. The logo on the bag was familiar, but I could not remember where I had seen it before. *Tinker and Tatler, Fine Antiques* was written in an old fashioned script on its front.

"Tinker's Tat," said Grandma later, as she dished out hot tea and sandwiches to the young, waterlogged policeman on board the *Fiona.* I was about to ask what she meant when she explained that many years ago, Mr Tinker and Mr Tatler had gone into partnership in the town. They had come from London, where they had owned a shop that sold antiques and aimed to do the same here. For a while, their shop was the best in town and people would come from miles around to buy their fine furniture, but Mr Tatler was homesick and went back to London. Having left Mr Tinker to run the shop, it soon became obvious who the brains behind the business had been. With Mr Tatler gone, Mr Tinker soon found himself struggling to make the shop pay. As the years passed, the fine antiques were replaced with junk and people began to refer to the shop as 'Tinker's Tat'.

“I heard that Mr Tinker had become so ill that he had sent for his nephew from London to run the shop, so perhaps things will improve.”
Despite the hot tea, the young policeman sneezed and shivered on the cockpit seat as water dripped from his hair and made a waterfall of the end of his nose.
“You’ll take a chill,” said Grandma and as if she was offering him a biscuit, he replied, “No thank you, I’ve already got one.” Everyone found this very amusing, which cheered him up, but I think he was pleased to see his sergeant return with a dry uniform.
As we watched the police officers drive away, Grandma looked thoughtfully at the carrier bag lying in the bottom of Bob’s boat and said,
"Tomorrow, we are going shopping for antiques.”

Chapter 9

Just before ten o'clock the next morning, we parked across the Town Square from *Tinker and Tatler, Fine Antiques* and waited. As the town clock sounded the hour, a hand appeared at the glass panel in the door of the shop and lifted the blind that covered it. The hand then turned the CLOSED sign round so that it read OPEN and slid back the bolts at the top and bottom of the door before opening it wide. The hand was followed by a lumpen body that belonged to an elderly man. He stood in the doorway and looked up and down the street before disappearing back inside the shop.

"Is that Mr. Tinker?" I asked as he reappeared, shuffling a battered garden table and chair onto the pavement.

"It is ... and it isn't," said Grandma. "That's Old Mr Tinker's nephew, who's also called Mr Tinker." I had expected him to be a young man, but was told that Old Mr Tinker was now in his eighties and so it seemed logical that his nephew must be about the same age as Grandma. We watched as he carried out a wicker cat basket with a hole in one side and placed it on the table.

"Something for Dotty," I joked.

A scruffy pair of fisherman's waders came out after that. "And something for P.C. Raines," chuckled Grandma.

Next, Young Mr Tinker brought out a threadbare deckchair and after having had some difficulty in making it stand up on its own, rested it against the shop wall. “Something for Billy O,” I said.
Finally, a large, stuffed, brown bear was positioned near the doorway, a bowler hat balanced on top of its head, a golf club in one paw and a small finger post with the words, ‘Extensive Showroom Inside. Come in and Browse’ in the other.
We looked at each other and spluttered. “Definitely something for The Danvers,” we said at the same time.
Young Mr Tinker seemed satisfied with his pavement display and retreated to the ‘Extensive Showroom’.
“Give him a few minutes,” said Grandma. “We want his full attention.”
When the town clock showed ten minutes past ten, we crossed the road, going first to the butcher's on the other side of the antique shop. Grandma bought some sausages, bacon and two lamb chops. As she left the shop, she pretended that she was going to walk straight past *Tinker and Tatler's,* but as we had rehearsed, I called her to come and look at an old doll in the window.
I played my part well, pleading with her to come and look inside.
“All right,” she said in a voice loud enough to be heard inside the shop, “but we can’t be long.”
‘Extensive Showroom’ was not how I would have described the shop, as piles of broken, incomplete or worn items towered above us on each side of the

entrance, leaving little room to 'Come In' or to 'Browse'. Heaps of books with torn covers and tattered comics; teapots with missing lids or broken spouts; hats, walking sticks and umbrellas loomed up on every side, blocking out the light and filling the air with a musty staleness. As my eyes grew accustomed to the gloomy interior, I spotted what I was looking for and cried out, "Look, Grandma, barometers!" I steered her towards a wall near to the back of the shop, where two banjo-style barometers were hanging.

"Too big, I think," said Grandma, playing her part. "They're definitely too big. It's quite a small space."

"Can I help you ladies?" Young Mr Tinker had crept up so silently that I jumped when he spoke. Close up, he was even more lumpy, with a carbuncle on his forehead and two warts on the end of his nose. The dim light made his skin look grey and clammy and he reminded me of a toad.

"I don't think so," said Grandma. "I need a barometer for my hallway. I bought one some years ago, but it needs replacing." This was what she often called, 'being selective with the truth', as she had bought a barometer some years ago, but it had never been in the hallway and it did not need replacing. It was next to the Captain's photograph onboard the *Fiona.* "These are much too big. What I need is just the barometer without the thermometer on top."

As she turned to leave, Young Mr Tinker hesitated for a moment and then took the bait, "I might have just what you're looking for," he said. "It came in yesterday, so I haven't had time to clean it yet. If you wouldn't mind waiting, I'll go and fetch it from the storeroom." We watched as he took a small key from a drawer behind the counter and unlocked a door at the back of the shop. He returned with a brass barometer mounted on a square wooden plinth and handed it to Grandma. She did not want to seem too eager, so tapped the glass and checked for scratches and dents. "Hmm," she pondered, "it might do. How much are you asking for it?"

Young Mr Tinker said that he could take no less than thirty pounds, as it was a very fine piece and in good working order.

"I think it would fit," she said, "but I would need to make sure. Could you write down the measurements? I can check the space and come back tomorrow morning if it is the right size. Do you mind putting it by?" Young Mr Tinker said that he would keep it until the next day and sorted through the draw behind the counter for a ruler and a piece of paper on which to write the measurements. While he was busy, Grandma turned the barometer over, nudging me so that I could see what she had spotted. Forming a perfect square on the back was a line of blue paint all around the edge.

We walked calmly back to the car and once inside, drove at top speed, not to Graymalkin Cottage or to the Old Harbour, but to the Police Station.

I was pleased to see that P. C. Raines was on the Reception desk, although his red nose and the box of

tissues at his elbow, told us that he had not fully recovered from his dip in the canal.
He smiled when he saw us. "Good news," he said. "The binoculars are engraved with Captain Danvers' name. What's more, they've managed to lift a fingerprint from them. Sadly there's no match on our database, so the thief hasn't been in trouble before..."
"Or perhaps he hasn't been caught!" said Grandma. "Well, I have some good news for you," she continued. "I know where you'll find the owner of your fingerprint!" She told the young policeman how we had gone "undercover", as she called it and "hoodwinked" the thief. I thought that she had been watching too many detective programmes on television, but P. C. Raines seemed impressed and called his sergeant, who in turn called the Detective Inspector. We were shown into an interview room, where we were questioned about what we had said and what we had seen. The Detective Inspector asked us not to return to the shop, as we could be in danger if Young Mr Tinker had accomplices or 'turned nasty', as he put it. He explained that he would need to get a warrant, which would give him permission to search the shop. He thanked us for being good citizens and promised to let us know the outcome of the investigation. I think that we were both disappointed that we would not be involved in the arrest, but drove to the Old Harbour and contented ourselves with a bacon sandwich on board the *Fiona.* The smell of the bacon cooking brought Bob to our boat, eager to know what had happened at *Tinker*

and Tatler's. Grandma had already explained to him that it was better if he did not come with us, as his family was well-known in the town, whereas she was not and so could be "incognito", whatever that was.
"The smell of this bacon must be traveling a long way," she said, nodding towards the car park, where P. C. Raines had pulled up in a police car. While he was walking round to the boat, she prepared another sandwich and soon we were all sitting on the deck enjoying our lunch. Between mouthfuls, P. C. Raines told us that he had been sent to let us know what had happened after we had left the police station.
"Young Mr Tinker knew that we were onto him as soon as we walked into the shop and straight away, he took us into his storeroom and showed us everything he'd stolen. To be honest, I think he was relieved that it was all over. He said that he had taken over the shop when his uncle had fallen ill and hadn't realised what a state it was in. There was no money in the bank and the stock was so shabby that nobody wanted to buy anything. It was then that he decided to burgle the boats. He said that it was easier than breaking into people's houses. I don't think he was very good at being a thief, because he'd not managed to sell a single thing that he'd stolen."
"That's good news," said Grandma. "At least everyone will get their things back."
"But why did he throw the binoculars away?" I asked.
"And why was the carrier bag in the water?" added Bob.

"He'd used a torch to get on board the boats, but he was so useless that the battery went as soon as he got onto *Dans Vers.* When he was outside the Old Harbour, he parked near to the oak tree to check what he'd got. Because the binoculars were engraved with Captain Danvers' name, he knew that they would be too easy to trace so he threw them into the canal. It was dark, so he didn't realise that they hadn't sunk and were still resting among the reeds. As for the carrier bag, it was quite windy that night and it blew out of his car and into the canal when he opened the door to get rid of the binoculars."
"Well," said Grandma, sad that we had not been there for the arrest, "we never did get to Derring Do!"
I laughed and added, "But I think that Young Mr Tinker will be in the town of Tribulation for some time to come!"
P. C. Raines looked bewildered,"What?" he questioned.
"Past the town of Tribulation and straight on to Derring Do!" I said and winking at Grandma I added, "Have you never heard that before?"
P. C.Raines shook his head, so I explained, "It means that you must put your troubles behind you and have fun!"
"That's one explanation," laughed Grandma, "and a good one at that!"

Chapter 10

Ma turned the pages of my log, sometimes laughing, sometimes gasping as the story unfolded. I had included a sketch map, showing the place where the binoculars and the carrier bag had been found. On one page, there was a description of *Tinker and Tatler, Fine Antiques,* showing Young Mr Tinker with a toad's head, but the page that I was most proud of made Ma roar with laughter. It showed P. C. Raines sitting in the reeds and was entitled, 'Wet by name and wet by nature'.

I had not been looking forward to our Friday visit, but here was the cheerful, lively Ma that I loved so much. The colour had returned to her cheeks and there was a twinkle in her eye. She also seemed to be less tired and suggested that we went for a walk after lunch. She held my hand as we walked down the street towards the town.

"Thank you for being so good about staying with Grandma. It's been really helpful, but I have missed you," she said. "You shouldn't have to stay for much longer. I have a visit to the hospital the week after next and if all goes well, you might be able to come home for the last two weeks of the holiday."

"Oh!" I said, trying to sound pleased.

"Only two more weeks at Graymalkin Cottage," I thought. "Only two more weeks of Grandma, Dotty, Billy O, Boat Boy Bob and the *Fiona*!"

I was so quiet on the drive back to my grandmother's house, that after about ten minutes she said, "A penny for them!"
"What?" I asked.
"A penny for your thoughts," she repeated.
I began slowly, "Ma says that I might be able to go home in two weeks time and ..."
"...and you don't want to go?" She didn't need to give me a penny for my thoughts, because she already knew them.
"Don't worry, she said cheerily. "There's still plenty of time for Derring Do!"
She could have had no idea how true her words would prove to be.
On Thursday of the third week of the holiday, it was becoming obvious that Grandma was planning something. A man met us at the *Fiona* and carried out a service on the engine, while Grandma, Bob and I hoisted the mainsail and checked it for damage.
"I found a wasps' nest in here after one winter," she explained as the great white sail flapped above us. Fortunately, except for a dead spider, there was nothing in the canvas this time.
"We'll have fish and chips in the clubhouse for supper tonight. I want to check the navigation lights when it starts to get dark," she said.
Perhaps it was the mention of fish, but Dotty sat up and stretched her long front legs, arched her back and peered over the boat's edge at the shoals of brown trout swimming by.

“Time for a swim,” said Grandma. The little cat chirped loudly at the sight of SMALL DOG, standing patiently as the straps were tightened under her belly. Her swim brought the usual crowd of onlookers with their cameras. They clapped as she swam backwards and forwards and cheered loudly as Grandma finally hoisted her back on board. After lunch, Bob and I rowed up the canal, returning to the Fiona at about two o’clock. There was still a lot of time until supper, so Grandma suggested that we took a tin of ‘Ship’s Biscuits’ to Billy O.

He was on Watch as usual, sitting in his chair and looking out onto the river. From time to time, he would lift his binoculars and scan from the bridges down stream up to the great Horseshoe Bend at Awre, sometimes stopping to focus on one spot when something caught his interest.

“What do you see out there?” I asked, wondering what could be so interesting day, after day.

“What do *you* see out there?” he asked.

I considered for a moment and then replied, “I see the river flowing past, seagulls on the sandbanks at low tide; I see the wind turbine on the opposite bank and a small yacht below the Severn Bridge.”

He seemed pleased with my reply. “Well, that’s more than most people see,” he said. “Now let me tell you what I see. I see the sands shifting day by day, and I take note of how the channel of safe passage changes slightly - not much, but enough to catch out an unwary sailor; I see the way the wind over tide whips up a maelstrom when the conditions are right

and I keep an eye on the silt building up behind the lock gates and let the Harbour Master know that he's going to have trouble getting them to open and close."
"Wow," said Bob, "Will you teach us about those things?"
Billy O laughed, "Let me tell you what else I see and then perhaps you'll understand what you will need to do if you want to learn about the ways of the water."
He paused for a moment and closed his eyes, "I see a young 'un - probably no older than you Gran'daughter - pushing his first dinghy down that slip. I see him five minutes later, upside down and scrambling to right his boat and get back on board," he chuckled. "I'd never been so wet in my life before, but I have been many times since," he continued. "I see a young man, taking cargo back and forth on the old trows until the river became too awkward and forced him to take passage round into the English Channel. In Portsmouth, he joined up and served for more than thirty years in the Royal Navy. I see that same man, but not so young now, coming home and taking his first yacht - about the same size as the *Fiona,* although not as pretty- up and down, in and out of the Old Harbour, until his old bones creaked and his lungs got too full of sea salt. Now I see an old man, who watches the river and is still learning about its awkward ways!"
Billy O seemed to be happy when he talked about the river and the sea, so I asked him to share some of his adventures. We lost track of time, as he told us

stories of storms in the North Sea and sharks in the Southern Ocean; of pirate attacks off Borneo and shipwrecks off Cape Horn and of walls of water that towered above the ship's bridge one minute and lifted you as high as a mountain, the next. As the sun sank low in the west, my head was so full of the pictures that he had painted of his life at sea, that I did not notice that Grandma had returned. As she parked near to the pier, she held up a carrier bag and called across to us, "Supper!"

Reluctantly, I left Billy O's tales of his fantastic adventures and ran to help my grandmother who was juggling car keys, fish and chips and Dotty's leash.

"Will you join us, William?" she asked. "There's plenty for everyone."

"Kind of you, Captain's Wife," he answered, "but I'd be keel hauled by the Chief Steward if I was late for my supper." Billy O lived with his sister and often joked that he was Master and Commander in all things, except the Galley, which was under her rule. The light was fading and he would soon make his way home to the cosy cottage they shared on the edge of the town.

Grandma, Bob, Dotty and I went up the narrow staircase of the old shipwright's house that now served as the clubhouse. From the window of an upstairs room we watched the water ebbing away down river and the exposed sandbanks glowing in the dying rays of the sun. After we had finished eating, we cleared the remnants of the meal and

were about to close the door and go downstairs, when the phone in the office began to ring.
Grandma hesitated for a moment at the top of the stairs. "Probably a wrong number," she said, moving onto the second step, but then something made her turn back.
We heard her answer, "The Yacht Club. Can I help you?" The cheerfulness left her voice and from the look on her face, we knew that something terrible had happened. "Oh no!" she exclaimed, "I'll do my best!"
Having replaced the receiver, she reached behind the door and took a key from the hook marked, 'Safety Boat Hut. Key MUST be returned after use'. She was trying to remain calm, but I could tell from the small tremor in her voice that she was anxious about something.
"Put Dotty in the car," she said to me. "I don't think she can join me on this voyage." As we went out into the harbour, she explained that the call had come from the Coastguard. He had told her that he had received a Mayday call from a yacht that had run aground about a hundred metres from the North pier. Lifeboats had been launched, but were about ten minutes away. He was concerned for the safety of the two people on board, as the tide was about to turn and was likely to sink their boat.
By now, we had reached the Safety Boat Hut on the edge of the slipway. Unfastening the padlock, Grandma ran her hand along the wall in search of a light switch.

"Life jackets," she said. "We need life jackets and I can't find them in the dark. There's a torch on the *Fiona,* but every second counts and there's no time to go and fetch it."

A noise like a toy trumpet came from the doorway, "Well it's a good job I'm here!" wheezed Billy O, as he reached above the door and flicked a switch. The neon strip flickered for a moment and then flooded the hut with light. As soon as we were wearing the life jackets, we set about launching the RIB that was used as the safety boat. It was less than five metres in length and sat on a trailer. Between the four of us, we managed to manoeuvre it to the top of the slipway.

"Phew," puffed Grandma, "how can something that's so full of air be so heavy?" As she did so, the trailer took off at a pace and the boat splashed into the small pool of water at the bottom of the slipway.

"All aboard," commanded Billy O.

"*You're* not coming," insisted Grandma.

"No time to argue, Captain's Wife. I don't see anyone here who knows this river as well as I do!" Turning to Bob and I he gave the order, "Young 'uns sit on the tubes and hold as tight as you can to the ropes!"

"*They're* not coming!" protested Grandma, but it was too late. With Captain William O'Donnell at the helm, the outboard motor roared into life and we headed out round the pier head. Almost immediately, we saw a forty-foot yacht, lying on its side on the sandbank on the other side of the harbour wall. In the twilight, she looked like a great, beached whale. Her hull faced towards us and we could just make out her keel, most of which had been buried when it sliced into the sands. *I.T.'s Mine* was written on the stern and Billy O shook his head and marvelled at the strange names people gave their boats nowadays. His had been called the *Lovely Molly* after a girl he had been sweet on when he was a boy.

As we drew close, he told Bob that he was going to turn the safety boat, so that it was facing back towards the pier and that he was to be ready to reach out and hold onto the yacht's keel to prevent us being swept back up river when the tide turned.

"Ahoy, there!" Billy O called out, when we were in position. "We've come to rescue you. Tie a mooring line onto one of your cleats and throw the other end down to the Captain's Wife here and she'll hold it steady."

It was almost dark now but, high above us we could see two pale faces peering nervously over the side.

"Heavens to Betsy, they've sent The Old Man of the Sea, his wife and two kids to rescue us. I think I'd rather stay put!" a man's voice said.

I thought that Billy O would have been offended by this, but instead called up, "Just be thankful that they didn't bring the cat!" He continued more seriously, "We've got a few minutes of slack water, then the tide will rush in and flood your boat."

I knew that slack water was the short time when the tide stood still before changing direction and I began to worry that when it did, it might push the large boat onto us.

"Couldn't you come round," a woman's voice said. " I could walk across the sand and get onto your boat more easily that way."
"Doesn't want to get her expensive deck shoes wet," muttered Billy O under his breath and then, not too patiently replied, "If I come round, I'll be stuck on the sand, and as for walking on it, it's not the French Riviera! You'd be up to your waist before you'd taken two steps!" This seemed to convince the woman that she might be safer doing as she was told and we watched as a mooring line was thrown over the side followed by two legs. Holding tightly to the rope, she shuffled down the hull and onto our boat, while Grandma held onto the other end of the line. Once on board, Billy O told her to sit next to me on the tube and act as ballast.
"Now you, sir," he shouted up to the man.
"I'll wait for the lifeboat," came the reply. "I can see its lights coming up the river."
There was a small gap between the keel and the sand, through which Bob had a view as far down as the bridges.
"They're quite a way off," he said to Billy O. "I reckon five to ten minutes."
At that moment, the water beneath us started to churn and Bob struggled to keep hold of the yacht's keel.
"The tide's turned," Billy O shouted up to the man. "It's now or never!" As he said this, the tide lifted the *I.T.'s Mine* a few inches, before slamming it back down onto the sand. This had the desired effect.

The man's legs appeared over the side and he scrambled frantically down the upturned hull and onto the safety boat.

Immediately, Billy O gave the command, "Right, Bob, push us off!"

Our boat was much heavier now, but his experience at the helm and his understanding of the tide and the sands soon brought us back round the pier head. The sight that greeted us was different from the one we had left. Lights blazed from every quarter, as cars had been brought to the top of the slipway, their headlights illuminating our passage. Many hands were ready to haul us out of the water when we reached the bottom of the slip, and a loud cheer went up as we came ashore. Apparently, after the Coastguard had spoken to Grandma, he had contacted the Harbour Master, who had in turn contacted the Commodore, who had in turn contacted everyone who lived nearby.

I recognised Mr Williamson, who had heard about the yacht on his radio and as he lived close by, was determined to get a "scoop" as he called it. He took photograph after photograph as we came ashore and then asked us to pose in front of the safety boat for one last shot. Grandma began frantically sorting through her pockets and then finding what she was looking for, applied a coat of bright red lipstick.

"Well," she said, winking at me, "a girl has to look her best!"

Suddenly, I remembered that we had left Dotty in the car and was worried that all the noise and commotion must be terrifying for the little cat. In the back window, I could see the silhouette of her head and two bright pinpoints of light reflected by her wide eyes.

"Wait for one minute," I said running to the car. I was greeted with a loud chirp, as I picked her up and carried her back to the safety boat.

"I might have guessed that she would not miss the chance to have her photograph taken," joked Mr. Williamson. Dotty sat on the prow of the boat with Grandma and Billy O on either side and Bob and I kneeling in front.

"Just like the Queen of Sheba!" said Grandma.

"Who's the ...", I started to say, but then looked at the little cat's regal pose and didn't need to ask.

Chapter 11

A loud cheer went up from the pier head, as a tall mast moved alongside the wall. Bob and I ran to join the crowd, watching as two of the crew from the lifeboat steered the *I.T.'s Mine* round to the jetty and tied up.

"Not enough water to bring her into the lock, yet," came a familiar voice from behind us. "I never thought that they would be able to get her upright again, which goes to prove that I still have a lot to learn about this water!" Billy O nodded in disbelief.

"Captain O'Donnell?" the Coxswain of the lifeboat had left his crew to secure the yacht and was walking towards us, his hand outstretched. "I would like to shake the hand of the finest sailor I've ever seen!'

Billy O thanked him, although he pointed out that no sailing had been involved.

"No sailing, but plenty of seamanship!' added the Coxswain. "I would consider it a great honour if you would allow me to buy you a tot of rum."

As we followed them back into the clubhouse, I whispered to Bob that now a tot of rum was concerned, Billy O seemed to have lost his fear of the Chief Steward.

The bar was full and a rousing three cheers went up as we stepped inside. The owners of the stricken yacht looked much happier now, having been provided with several cups of tea by Grandma. Dotty

was sitting on the woman's lap and allowing herself to be stroked and fussed.
"I'm sorry if I was rude to you out there." The owner of the *I.T's Mine* seized Billy O's hand and shook it so hard that I thought it might fall off. "To be honest, we were both delighted to see you arrive. I don't think that either of us realised how much danger we were in until we looked back at our boat from the harbour wall."
He explained that they had been heading for Sharpness, but had misjudged their timings and while trying to find enough water to stay afloat in the narrow channels, had ran aground.
"Time and Tide wait for no man," said Billy O, wisely.
"And not many women either," added Grandma, " and it's time I took these children home."
I was sorry to leave the club, as it had become alive with old sailors and young sailors swapping stories of the times they had waited for the tide while sitting on a sandbank. Tales of high seas and low water grew with the telling, so that three foot waves became 'as high as a house'.
Grandma said that it was too late for Bob to ride home, so she suggested that he loaded his bicycle into the back of the Land Rover and she would give him a lift. When we arrived at his house, Grandma said that it would probably be a good idea if she talked to his mother about what had happened. I watched as Bob disappeared around the side of the house with his bicycle, while Grandma stood on the doorstep, telling his mother about the evening's

adventures. When she returned to the car, she was smiling broadly.
"That's sorted, then!" she said. I thought that she was pleased that she had been able to explain everything to Bob's mother without her getting cross with him for being so late. I was later to find out that the rescue was not the only thing they had been talking about!
I was feeling sleepy now and snuggled into the car seat, lulled by the purr of the engine, until I was shaken awake as we rattled over the potholes in the lane that led to Graymalkin Cottage.
Later, when she came into my room to say goodnight, I said sleepily, "Grandma, I think we went to Derring Do, tonight."
"And did you like it there?" she asked.
I gave no answer, because I was already dreaming of adventures on the high seas.

I woke next morning to the sound of Grandma's voice in the next room.
"She's still asleep," she said. "It was exhausting for all of us!
I gradually became aware that she was on the phone to someone and guessed it must be Ma, because she finished with, "So it's all sorted. We'll see you at one o'clock."
I started to doze off again and then realised that today was Friday and we usually arrived at my house at midday. I looked at my watch and saw that it was almost ten-thirty. My grandmother appeared in the doorway of my bedroom, alerted by banging and

clattering as I opened drawers and cupboards, laying out what I would wear and then changing my mind. I almost ran into her on my way to the bathroom.

"Hold your horses!" she said. "Where's the fire?" She said that there was no need to hurry, as we were setting out slightly later today, so that I could have a rest after last night's adventure. "Besides," she said, "you might want to watch this."

She took me into her bedroom and turned on a small television set in the corner of the room. A voice announced, "Now here is the local news. Last night, two people were rescued from a yacht that had run aground in the River Severn...." I watched in amazement as mobile phone videos of the rescue and an interview with the lifeboat Coxswain were shown.

"Close your mouth, dear. It's not a pretty sight," said Grandma.

I clamped my jaw shut as I heard the Coxswain say that it was the most impressive bit of seamanship he had ever seen. The owner of the yacht was interviewed next. He was smartly dressed in a suit and tie and the words, 'Ian Tomkins, Director of The Information Technology Mine' appeared at the bottom of the screen and I suddenly understood why his boat had such an unusual name. He spoke about how grateful he was for the assistance he had been given, especially from Captain William O'Donnell and his crew. The news item finished with a still photograph of the four of us in front of the safety boat, with the

'Queen of Sheba' on the prow. It was an image I was to see many times that day.

There was hardly enough room for us to eat our breakfast, as the kitchen table was piled high with newspapers containing the same photograph.

"That newsagent will be able to retire if we carry on like this," said Grandma. The photograph we had just seen on television, was on the front cover of the *Clarion,* as well as inside many of the national papers. She had ordered extra copies for Ma, Aunt Hattie and, of course, my log and before we left the house we packed them into the car.

I was glad that we had taken so many, because Ma wanted to know everything and asked question after question, so it took twice as long to tell about the rescue than it had actually taken. We looked at all the photographs in the newspapers and read each report, at least twice! Finally satisfied that she had the whole story clear in her head, she declared that she was very proud of her mother and of her daughter. While I went through the whole story again with Aunt Hattie, Ma and Grandma went into the garden, where they seemed to be deep in conversation. I had reached the point in my log where the Coxswain offered Billy O a tot of rum, when they came in and said that they had a special announcement to make.

Ma began, "On Saturday, there is a rally at Portishead Marina. There will be music and stalls and boats of all shapes and sizes will visit. Would you like to go?"

"Yes, please!" I said, not needing to be asked twice. "Will we go in Grandma's car?"
Grandma continued, "No, in fact we will not go in a car at all!" I struggled to understand what she could mean, but hoped that we would not have to walk there!
"The only walking involved will be to and fro on the deck!" she said. She explained that Billy O's great-nephew, Alex, was home from university and was an excellent sailor, having been trained from an early age by Captain O'Donnell himself. "Bob will be coming with us, too," she added. I realised that her long conversation with his mother on the night of the rescue must have been about this. I could not believe that my dream of sailing was about to come true.

Chapter 12

A light breeze filled the sails as we locked out of the Old Harbour on Saturday morning. Alex O'Connell soon proved that he had the same salt water running in his veins, as that in his great-uncle's, as he tacked back and forth while Grandma plotted our course. In less than three hours we had reached Portishead and locked in. The marina was full of colour and noise. Boats were decked out in signal flags and a jazz band was playing happy, summer music on a small stage. Our berth was near to the Square where all the activity seemed to be and Grandma commented how lucky we had been to have been given such an excellent spot. I thought I saw her wink at Alex, as she said this, but it could have been that the sun was in her eyes. As we stepped ashore, I spotted Ma and Auntie Hattie. It seemed that they had been lucky too, as they had managed to get a table very near to the stage. When Dotty had been strapped into SMALL DOG and her leash attached, we made our way to their table. We had been sitting down for no more than five minutes, when a man approached our table and asked if someone called Bob was with us.
"There's a call for you in the Harbour Master's Office," he said and asked if Bob could go there as quickly as possible. Bob looked worried, so I offered to go with

him. The Office was on the first floor of a large glass-fronted building that overlooked the lock.
"I hope nothing's happened to Mum," he said as he bounded up the stairs, two at a time and I attempted to keep up with him. The Harbour Master beckoned to us to join him at glass window from where he oversaw movements in and out of the lock, far below.
"Just in time," he said and right on cue, we heard the radio crackle and a voice say, "Portishead Marina, this is the yacht *Morning Star* requesting lock in."
Bob swallowed hard, barely able to believe his ears. He tentatively peered down into the narrow passage that led to the lock. He listened again as he heard the Harbour Master give permission for the yacht to proceed and watched as the signal lights turned green, white and green.
And then a familiar boat came into view: the *Morning Star* rounded the pier and made her way down the narrow channel towards the entrance. By now, Bob had raced out of the office, down the stairs and was standing at the top of the lock gates. As I reached his side, I could see that the tall figure of a man was standing at the bow, mooring lines coiled in his hand. I recognised Bob's mother at the stern, but the greatest surprise was the figure on the helm. He raised his Breton cap in salute, giving the breeze the opportunity to ruffle his white whiskers, as he called up to me, "Ahoy, Gran'daughter!" After the boat had passed through the lock, Bob and I ran ahead until the *Morning Star* reached her mooring.

As we were tying up, I heard Bob ask his father, "Are you back ..."

... for good!" said his father, explaining that he had missed his family too much to stay away any longer. Bob hugged his father and mother and then we made our way back to the Square, where my family was waiting. Extra chairs were placed round our table and we made a happy, friendly group enjoying the afternoon sun.

After a while, the band stopped playing and a number of chairs were placed on the stage. A man stepped up to the microphone and welcomed everyone to this special event. He introduced the first guest as, "Mrs Tranter, the Head of Tourism South West" and a smartly dressed woman came to the front of the stage.

"Each year," began Mrs Tranter, "it is my pleasant duty to present an award to the individual who has brought the greatest number of visitors to any tourist attraction in our region. This year, there was a clear winner," she paused and turned towards our table. "I would like to ask Dotty the Swimming Cat to come forward and receive her award!"

Grandma carefully lifted the little cat, who was dozing peacefully on a chair, and carried her towards the stage. She placed her on a small table that had been put there for that purpose. The audience clapped loudly and several people got to their feet and shouted out, 'Bravo'. As Mrs Tranter hung a gold medal around Dotty's neck, the cat gave a loud chirp,

which brought more cheers and a good deal of laughter from the audience.
The woman smiled and said, "I didn't expect a speech from our winner, but it goes to prove what a great asset Dotty is to the Old Harbour!"
As the cameras captured the presentation, the cat sat upright, tilting her regal nose slightly, so that her subjects would know that she was in charge.
"Just like the..." I started to say to Bob.
"Queen of Sheba!" he completed the sentence.
Grandma and Dotty returned to their seats, as the man stepped forward again, thanked Mrs Tranter and announced that the next guest was the Chief Constable. A tall man in uniform came to the microphone.
"The job of the police force is made difficult by criminals," he began, "but occasionally, a member of the public comes forward to assist us in catching a wrongdoer. In this case, three members of the public became detectives and helped us to track down a thief, who has since been arrested," he said. "Something that is of little worth to a thief can be of great importance to its owner. It can have a personal value and can never be replaced. For this reason, before making the presentation I would like to ask Miss Eleanor Danvers to say a few words."
I had not noticed The Danvers sitting at the back of the stage, but now she appeared carrying a small red cushion, which she placed on the table before beginning to speak.

"When my boat was broken into, two things were stolen that - as the Chief Constable has said - had a special value to me. The thief took a barometer and some binoculars that had been given to me by my father. I thought that they had been lost for ever, and they would have been if it had not been for the actions of three people," she paused and looked across at our table, "two of whom are wonderful role models for young people."

As she read out our names, Grandma, Bob and I went onto the stage to receive our "Good Citizen" awards from the Chief Constable. He shook our hands, as he presented a scroll and a medal to each of us in turn. Grandma made a little speech, saying that it was the duty of each and every citizen to do what they knew to be right and then we returned to our table.

"Finally," said the man, " I would like to call on Coxswain Andrew Lawrence to make our final presentation."

I had last seen the Coxswain two days earlier, when he had shaken Billy O's hand and congratulated him on his seamanship, but now the dry suit, life jacket and wellingtons had been replaced by a smart navy blue jacket with two rows of brass buttons down the front and a white-topped hat.

"I wonder how many of us would put to sea in an attempt to save lives, especially on a tricky stretch of water in darkness," he began. "Well, that's exactly what one group of people did earlier this week." He

went on to tell the story of the rescue of the crew of the *I.T.'s Mine* and then said,
"I would like to present this award for bravery and exceptional seamanship to Captain William O'Donnell, Royal Navy, retired and for his crew." He called out our names and we went onto the stage again.
"I know how a yo-yo feels," said Grandma as she got up from her seat again, but I could tell that she was overjoyed to be at the centre of so much attention. After the presentation, we posed as a group, so that photographs could be taken. From the stage, I looked at Ma and Aunt Hattie, who were wiping tears of happiness from their eyes; I looked at Bob's mother and father who were glowing with pride; I looked at Billy O, full of dignity and self respect and I looked at Dotty ... who had fallen asleep again.
I could not remember a time when I had been so happy and tried to put the fact that I would soon have to return home, out of my head.
As the sun was setting, Ma and Aunt Hattie said that they must leave soon, as they were not staying on a boat and had a long journey home.
"Then you'd better tell her now," prompted Grandma.
"Very well," said Ma. "Grandma has suggested that instead of you coming home for the last two weeks before the new term begins, I come to stay with her. After all, I haven't had a holiday this year. I don't know how you feel about it and I'll understand if you don't want to ..." She never got to finish the sentence, because I had jumped up and hugged her so tightly

that she could hardly breathe. This was the perfect end to the day. The afternoon had been filled with music and games and we went to our beds, tired but happy. I was almost asleep, when I heard the cabin door open and through half-closed eyes, saw Grandma creep in. For a moment, she stood in front of the photograph of 'The Captain', before carefully hanging her medals above the picture frame. She gave a satisfied nod and whispered, "Well Andrew, wasn't that the cat's pyjamas?" before returning to her cabin.

Chapter 13

At twenty to nine, on the first Tuesday of September, Ma and I set out on the short walk from home to school. She was wearing a delicate, floral dress and had piled her hair into a neat bun on top of her head. When I told her how lovely she looked, she gave my hair a final brush, straightened my tie and said that I didn't look too bad myself.

"What are all these people doing outside the school gate?" I asked when we arrived. A large crowd had gathered on the pavement. Everyone was peering over each others shoulders as they struggled to see what was happening in the playground.

"Probably new parents waving goodbye to their little ones," she replied.

"She's here!" a loud whisper went through the crowd, as someone recognised me. People started to shuffle aside, clearing a pathway down which we were able to walk into the school grounds. Ahead of us, I could see the Headteacher standing next to the man from Breakfast Television who had signed my book at the festival. I puzzled for a moment about what I could have done to attract so much attention. I hadn't been involved with any more swimming cats; I hadn't helped catch any more thieves and I definitely hadn't rescued any more shipwrecked sailors. Then I saw Ian Tomkins, the captain of the *I.T.'s Mine.* He was telling the man from Breakfast Television that he had

wanted to thank the people who had saved him and as his company specialised in Information Technology, this seemed a good way of doing so.
The interviewer turned to the Headteacher next, who said that the gift would make a tremendous difference to her pupils. I was aware of a camera following me as the man from Breakfast Television beckoned to me to come and stand next to him.
"Well, the young lady in question has joined us just in time for the unveiling," he said, "but first, perhaps you would like to tell us a little about the rescue."
Remembering what I had written in my log, I gave a good account of the events of that evening. Occasionally, he would interrupt my story with questions, such as, "Were you frightened?" and, "Would you do it again?", which I answered as honestly as I could before continuing with my story.
As I finished, he turned to the camera and said,"Join us again after the Weather Forecast, when we will see exactly how Megan's bravery has been rewarded."
There was a flurry of activity as the cameras were moved to the far end of the playground, where a large blue curtain had been hung over the door of what had been the P.E. store.
A few minutes later, the interviewer turned to the camera and said, "Welcome back. Before the break we heard how Megan Waterfield, a ten year old girl, took part in a daring rescue at sea. Now, Mr Ian Tomkins, the man she rescued would like to invite her to unveil his special gift to her school."

Mr Tomkins made a short speech about how grateful he was for the way in which I had helped him and handed me the end of a long cord that was attached to the top of the curtain, inviting me to pull it. As the curtains parted, a gasp went up from the crowd, followed by a round of applause. Above the freshly painted door, a sign read, 'The Megan Waterfield Information Technology Suite'. On cue, the doors were opened by two members of staff who had been waiting inside. The old store had been freshly painted and fitted out with new workstations, banks of computers and a trolley containing laptops and tablets.

The Headteacher thanked Mr Tomkins on behalf of the school and the interview came to an end. The man from Breakfast Television said that he was now going to Bob's school where the same generous gift had been made, but as Bob did not want a fuss to be made, they were just going to interview the Headteacher.

"Teenagers!" he said as he left and for a moment, it reminded me of how Miss Danvers used to be.

When the camera crew had left, the playground returned to normal, except for the fact that no-one told me about *their* holidays this year, as they all wanted to hear about *mine*.

At ten o'clock, in the middle of our English lesson, the classroom door opened and Monty Moira came in with the school secretary, who explained that Moira's plane had been delayed. She had not arrived back from Barbados until after midnight, so her parents had allowed her to sleep late.

"Take a seat next to Megan," said the teacher. "She'll explain what to do. You have some catching up to do!"

As soon as Moira sat down, she was keen to show me her tan. After she had whispered about the people she had met, the clothes she had bought, and how dreadful the flight home had been, she asked, "And what did you do this year?"

I paused for a moment and said, "Oh, nothing much, but I did go past the Town of Tribulation and straight on to Derring Do!"

Made in the USA
Charleston, SC
13 August 2016